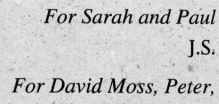

For Sarah and Paul
J.S.

For David Moss, Peter,
Mum and Dad
T.L.

Reprinted 1997, 1998

This paperback edition published 1996

First published in 1996 by Magi Publications
22 Manchester Street, London W1M 5PG

Text © 1996 Julie Sykes
Illustrations © 1996 Tanya Linch

Julie Sykes and Tanya Linch have asserted their rights
to be identified as the author and illustrator of this work
under the Copyright, Designs and Patents Act, 1988.

Printed and bound in Italy by Grafiche AZ, Verona

ISBN 1 85430 131 4

MAGI PUBLICATIONS

London

This and That

by Julie Sykes

illustrated by Tanya Linch

Down on the farm Cat woke early.
It was a special day and
she had work to do.

Horse was grazing in the field when
Cat jumped onto the fence.

'Hello, Horse,' said Cat. 'May I borrow
your stable?'
Horse didn't use his stable in the summer
because he liked to sleep outside.
'Yes,' he neighed. 'What will
you use it for?'
'This and that,' purred Cat.

Pig was rolling in his sty
when Cat leapt onto the wall.

'Hello, Pig,' said Cat. 'May I have some
of your straw?'
The farmer had just made Pig's bed.
The straw was clean and fresh and there
was plenty of it.
'Help yourself,' grunted Pig. 'What's it for?'
'This and that,' purred Cat.

Goat was playing in the yard when
Cat hopped on the gate and meowed.

'Hello, Goat,' said Cat.
'May I have some hay?'
Goat never ate hay in the
summer when the grass was green and lush.
'If you want,' he cried. 'Whatever do you
need it for?'
'This and that,' purred Cat.

Sheep was dozing under a leafy tree
when Cat climbed onto a branch.

'Hello, Sheep,' said Cat. 'May I have some of your soft wool?'
Sheep had a thick white coat and she had plenty to spare.
'Of course you may,' she bleated. 'What are you going to do with it?'
'This and that,' purred Cat.

Hen was scratching for grain when Cat leapt on top of the hen house.

'Hello, Hen,' said Cat.
'May I have a few of your
 feathers?'
Hen stopped scratching and
cocked her head curiously.
'You may,' she clucked.
'But whatever for?'
'This and that,' purred Cat.

Cow was drinking from the stream
when Cat joined her on the bank.

'Hello, Cow,' said Cat. 'May I have a few hairs
from your tail?'
Cow had a long tail with a hairy tip for swotting flies.
'Yes,' she mooed. 'What are you going to do with them?'
'This and that,' purred Cat.

Donkey was looking for thistles
when Cat jumped on his back.

'Hello, Donkey,' said Cat.
'May I borrow that lovely
purple ribbon from your hat?'
Donkey wore a hat to keep the sun out of his eyes. It was
decorated with a bright purple ribbon round the brim.
'If you're careful with it,' he said. 'What do you
want it for?'
'This and that,' purred Cat.

The animals thought Cat was behaving strangely.
'What does she want with all our things?' clucked Hen.
'Perhaps she's moving house,' mooed Cow.
'No,' grunted Pig. 'Cats don't like moving.'
'Let's follow her,' brayed Donkey.

The animals all hid in
the yard, and when Cat
appeared they tiptoed
after her.

Cat went inside the stable and the
animals followed silently behind.

In one corner they saw . . .

. . . two little kittens.

They were inside a nest
made from hay and straw.
It was lined with
Sheep's wool,
hair from Cow's tail and
feathers from Hen.
It was decorated with
Donkey's pretty purple
ribbon.

'What a lovely surprise,'
neighed Horse.
'They're beautiful,' said Goat.
'So that's what you needed our
things for!' exclaimed Sheep.
Leaning over the huge nest,
Donkey asked, 'What are
they called?'
Cat sighed. 'I don't know,
I can't decide. What do you think?'
The animals looked at each other.

Then together they

neighed and grunted,

bleated and clucked,

hee-hawed and mooed,

'WE KNOW . . .

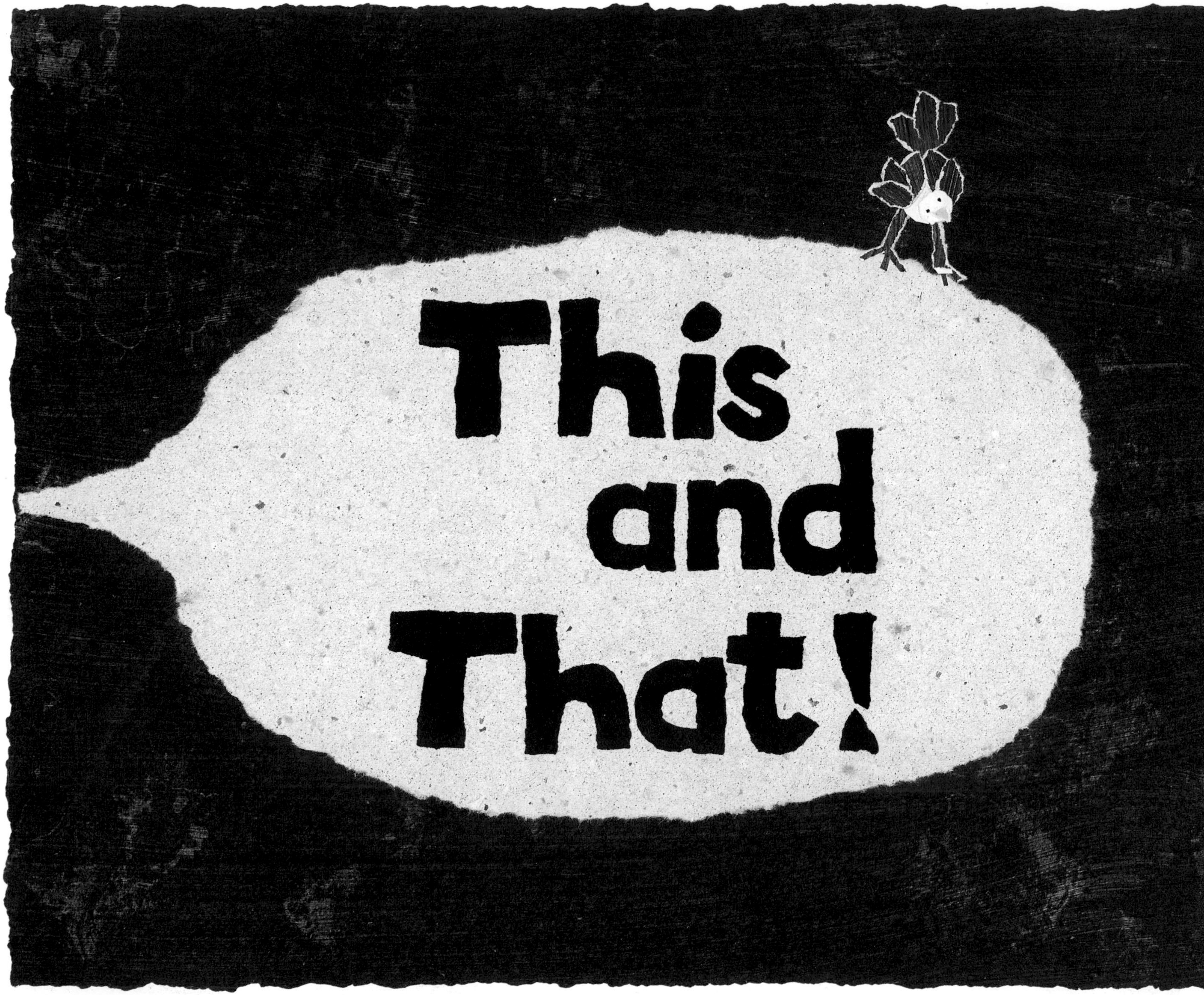
This
and
That!